T0123545

Trouble
or
Success

Trouble
or
Success

Keishawn Charles

iUniverse

TROUBLE OR SUCCESS

iUniverse books may be ordered through booksellers or by contacting:

iUniverse
1663 Liberty Drive
Bloomington, IN 47403
www.iuniverse.com
1-800-Authors (1-800-288-4677)

Because of the dynamic nature of the Internet, any web addresses or links contained in this book may have changed since publication and may no longer be valid. The views expressed in this work are solely those of the author and do not necessarily reflect the views of the publisher, and the publisher hereby disclaims any responsibility for them.

Any people depicted in stock imagery provided by Getty Images are models, and such images are being used for illustrative purposes only. Certain stock imagery © Getty Images.

ISBN: 978-1-5320-4307-9 (sc)
ISBN: 978-1-5320-4308-6 (e)

Library of Congress Control Number: 2018902012

Print information available on the last page.

iUniverse rev. date: 03/14/2018

Dedication

Mom I know you can't hear me but I want to say I miss you and I love you. Your daughter is doing good and Bert she's doing good to, I wanted to let you know we are all doing fine and yea mom your baby boy did it he's successful now I always said that now I'm doing. It was a Lil hard at first but I got it done. Mom I love and I miss you talk soon love you.

Derek and Chris are two friends that grew up on the same block in, New Orleans, Louisiana, with a dream to make it out. Both of their Mothers worked two jobs to make a better life. However New Orleans was a very dangerous city and one Bad decision could cost you. So Derek and Chris knew they had to make it out. Derek and Chris Were both very smart boys. Derek didn't really care for school as much as Chirs did. So One day while they were Chilling Derek says to Chris, " Yo I think we should play sports"..What sport should we play? Football, the only way Derek stay in school, so as they go on Chris and Derek went on through school, and to graduate school and earning scholarships to Howard University.

As Chris and Derek are just under nine weeks before to they go off To Howard Derek gets his longtime girlfriend Ashley pregnant. She Can't Believe what she is seeing right now Shocked Scared and nervous She Calls Derek after Who's just finishing his workout with Chris. Ashley tells him she is 7 weeks pregnant, Automatically assumes it's a joke so Derek laughs and asks "You're joking Right? Offended due to her Hormones Ashley says hell no I`m not joking!!! Now its Derek's Turn to have an attitude because he knows girls will try anything to get out of them Projects It`s not mine Ashley!!! starts screaming and yelling saying I havent been with nobody but you. So Derek say`s we will see when the

DNA, come back because you know you been passed around. So four week`s go by and Ashley and Derek says he knows a doctor that cant perform a dna test while she's still pregnant. He's Glad Medicaid pays for couldn't afford the price. Two weeks later their DNA test Results come back and Derek is 99.9 percent the father so that`s when Derek made his mind up that he was gone to be the best father he could because he know that he could not make the same bad decisions that his dad made. So Derek went and has a talk with Ashley mom Mrs. Sandra and Mrs. Mary Her grandmom about his unborn child. Mrs. Sander said how do you plan to support your child Derek says he will not go to college instead I will get a job, so her Ashley grandmother told him no you not do that go ahead to college, but when you come home you will, get your child and if you don`t she will put you on child support. So all things were going in a good direction for Chris and Derek, but what came they way next will determine their future and especially for Chris. Then it`s appends Chris mom is walking home from work one night and drive by shooting take place, and his mother dies.

How Derek found out Chris and Derek was at his house playing maddened. When they hear a knock at the door and Chris asked "who is it"? The police said, "Open the door we have to talk to you." so Chris opens the door and the cops told him his mother has been murdered. At this moment Chris is in shock his mother has been killed and Derek said,"Are y'all for real like stop playing?". The cops said, we are not playing and Chris breaks down and loses it. Now all this happened Right before they left for college. So Chris said, do you know who did it? The cops Said no, But We will do everything they can, So the day after his mom funeral Chris tell Derek he found out who killed

his mom and he was taking matters into his own hands.

Therefore Derek is trying to be there for his friend but Chris keep, pushing him away and Derek and his mom try to tell him don't make the biggest mistake of your life and, I ruin it before it gets started. So Derek mom said,"Ya'll bow y'all heads and let's pray. God we come to you and this horrific time, in our life's as we have lost someone very special and close to us, God we are asking you to keep Chris and Derek close to the kingdom because we know that Sherry is watching over them in Jesus name we pray amen, amen and amen.

So Derek look over at Chris, and see he still's has that look in his eyes, Chris gets up and Derek know Chris was about to make a terrible decision. Chris walk out of the house Derek tryst to run him down, but Chris pulls away from Derek and tells him to stay away from him, so as Chris walk further away from him and he goes back in the house and a hour later Chris hears gun shots. Derek get's up and run out of the house, he runs to the next block but by the time he got there it was too late. The police had Chris surrounded, him with their, guns and Derek know he couldn't save him as Chris had done so many times for him. So Chris was charged with attempted murder and position of a firearm and

he was sentenced to fifteen years in federal prison without the possibility of parole.

Now with Chris being in prison for the next fifteen years Derek had to be strong and still go to college, his child being on the way here. Derek go on to college to play football, he played two years at Howard University and went pro, and being drafted to the Pittsburg Steelers, as the 10th pick overall . So Ashley his longtime girlfriend had a baby boy by the name of Derek Jones Jr and him Ashley went on to get married and have two more kids and every off season he went too see Chris and Derek was released after eights years for good behavior.

Chris was out of prison but Chris was to far gone and he went two the streets and Derek is trying too help Chris but it's to late. So that's when Derek know he had too separate himself Chris so as they separate Chris has falling more and more into the streets and they was nothing Derek could about it.The years went own and at this point Derek and Chris are living too different lifes, so one night Chris and his crew was about to go rob a drug dealer and when they get their, Chris kicks in the door run too the back open the safe turns around and get's killed by Eric and Shawn the too he took with him and now they are the kings of the block.So how Derek found out was Derek's mom called him

crying why he was home with his wife and kids and broke down crying and told his mom that he was trying too call Chris all day and last night, so the next day Derek and Ashley and the kids flew back too New Orleans to pay respect to his falling friend he had lost, and Chris had four children,Derek paid for the funeral and his kids college and more and his kids too, and they mothers and niece homes.

So that's go two show you that if you make the wrong choices in life that's the kind of thing's can happened I tell this story because I want you to think befor you make a decision that can change your life,look at chirs and Derek for and example one went right and the other went left. So keep god first and pray every day and god will bring you throw it all The year's went own and Derek was still trying two deal with the def of his firend thinking he could had take two chirs a little bit more. So fro first time in five years Derek visit he's best firend grave since he died. But what people don't know is afther Derek visit the grave Derek went in to depression and anxiety then to months later he stared poping pills.

One night Derek Awoke from his sleep and has a seizure foaming at the mouth his wife jumps up and called 911 and they rushed him two the hospital. Derek and his wife get's to the hospital he was put on life support for 8 days his wife notified the team and they notified the NFL. After life support Derek check in the rehab and he was suspended from the NFL for a year. But after a year in rehab and suspended from the NFL he got his second shot in life and the NFL gave him a second chance at his NFL life, and he was signed to the RAMS. He want on to play four more years and retired at the age of 37 years old. You see this story was told to

help someone get throw what every they going throw and remember god can bring you throw anything, keep god first and you get will get to the other side.